Mrs. Claus's Crazy Christmas

by Steven Kroll

illustrated by John Wallner

Holiday House / New York

Library of Congress Cataloging in Publication Data

Kroll, Steven.
    Mrs. Claus's crazy Christmas.

    Summary: Mrs. Claus has an adventure on Christmas
Eve when she delivers a puppy Santa left behind.
    1. Children's stories, American. [1. Christmas—
Fiction] I. Wallner, John C., ill. II. Title.
III. Title: Mistress Claus's crazy Christmas.
PZ7.K9225Mr 1985   [E]   84-25218
ISBN 0-8234-0563-X

IT WAS CHRISTMAS EVE. Santa Claus was getting ready to leave the North Pole. He checked his bag of presents. He hitched up the last of his reindeer and jumped into his sleigh.

"Ho, ho, ho!" he laughed. "See you later, Mrs. Claus."

Mrs. Claus waved until the sleigh was just a small spot in the sky. Then she went inside.

Santa's elves were sleeping everywhere. They were very tired from making so many presents.

"Come on, guys," said Mrs. Claus. "Can't we do something fun?"

No one moved or spoke. "Zzzzzzzzz" was all Mrs. Claus heard.

"Hmph," she muttered. "It's never any fun around here Christmas Eve."

She sat down and tried to read.

"Thump, thump, thump!" she heard. "Yip, yip, yip!"

"What's that?" said Mrs. Claus.

She stood up. A little brown-and-white puppy ran across the living room.

Mrs. Claus scooped him into her arms. She read the tag around his neck. "For Davey," it said.

"Oh, my goodness," said Mrs. Claus. "Santa has forgotten Davey's present! What ever shall I do?"

She walked up and down, talking to herself. Suddenly she had an idea. *"I'll* take Davey his present," she said. "Why should Santa have all the fun?"

Mrs. Claus went to the bedroom. She pulled out Santa's old Santa suit and put it on. The sleeves were too long, and the seat was baggy.

"Well, it's much too big, but it will have to do," she said.

She picked up the puppy and went out to the shed. Santa's old sleigh was buried under a lot of gift boxes. Its paint was chipped, but it was still in good shape.

Next she went to the barn. Dixon, Santa's oldest reindeer, was asleep in his stall. He'd been retired for so long, people didn't even know his name.

"Dixon," said Mrs. Claus, "I need your help. Would you pull Santa's old sleigh tonight?"

Dixon kicked up his heels and ran to the sleigh. Mrs. Claus rushed after him and hitched him up.

She put the puppy down beside her on the seat. Then they zoomed into the sky, just missing the chimney of the house.

They flew higher and higher. The stars twinkled all around them. It got colder.

Mrs. Claus pulled down the earflaps of Santa's old hat. She put the puppy in her lap to keep him warm.

It began to snow. Big, soft flakes drifted slowly by. But the snow got heavier, and the wind came up. The flakes whirled around so much, it was hard to see.

Mrs. Claus and Dixon flew on. And on. And on.

But Dixon was getting tired. The sleigh began to dip.

"Dixon!" said Mrs. Claus. "Be careful. Oh, goodness."

They could see a town below them now. The roofs and spires rose up out of the snow.

"Dixon!" said Mrs. Claus. "Aim for that flat roof!"

Dixon aimed and missed. The sleigh bumped to the ground.

"Goodness," said Mrs. Claus. "We're in the middle of the street!"

People were passing by. Some of them were coming back from church.

"Look!" said a little girl. "There's Santa Claus!"

"I don't believe it," said her father.

"Oh, my goodness," said Mrs. Claus. "I'm going to be seen."

She grabbed the puppy. "Dixon, watch the sleigh. I'll be right back."

She dashed across the street and hid in a doorway. The father and daughter reached the sleigh.

"Where has Santa gone?" asked the little girl.

"He's got to be around somewhere, Millie," said her father.

Millie and her father raced across the street, looking for Santa. They passed the doorway where Mrs. Claus was hiding.

Suddenly the puppy jumped out of Mrs. Claus's arms. "Oh, goodness!" she said, and ran after him.

The puppy barked twice and streaked past Millie and her father.

"Look, a puppy!" said Millie.

"Look, Santa!" said her father as Mrs. Claus raced by.

The two of them ran after Mrs. Claus, shouting. Soon a whole crowd was chasing her.

It was hard to run in Santa's old clothes, but Mrs. Claus huffed and puffed and kept going. The puppy was less than half a block ahead when he disappeared through an open door.

Mrs. Claus rushed after him. The room was filled with
people singing carols. The puppy dashed through lots of legs
and hid under the sofa.

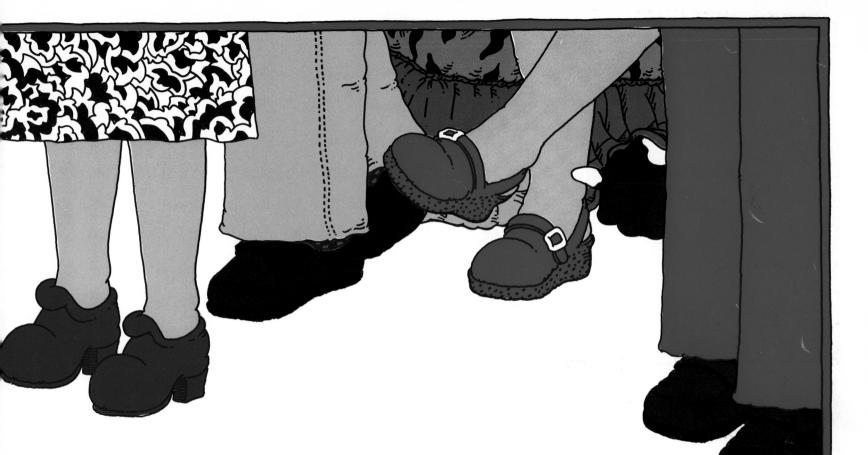

Mrs. Claus struggled after him. "Excuse me," she said,
"excuse me."

"Hey, there's Santa!" someone said.

"Look, Santa's arrived!" said someone else.

Mrs. Claus pulled the puppy out from under the sofa,
opened the nearest window, and jumped through.

"Bad puppy," she said as she ran back toward the sleigh.

The puppy licked her nose.

Dixon and the sleigh were right where she'd left them. "To Davey's," she said, and jumped on board.

Dixon took off. The sky was clear now, and the moon was out. They flew for miles. Finally they came to Davey's house. They landed with a bump on the roof.

Mrs. Claus took the puppy and tumbled down the chimney. She bumped down into the fireplace.

"Oh, goodness," she said. She brushed off some ashes and left the puppy under the Christmas tree.

Suddenly she heard a voice: "Who's down there?"

A door slammed. Someone was coming!

Mrs. Claus dashed out the front door. She climbed up to the roof and collapsed in the sleigh. "On Dixon!" she shouted.

They headed for home—over the roofs of the world while everyone slept.

Hours later, they reached the North Pole. As they landed, Mrs. Claus saw Santa's sleigh parked in the shed. The reindeer were back in their stalls.

"Oh, my goodness," she said. "Santa's home already. What's he going to say?"

Suddenly the front door flew open. There stood Santa.

"Mrs. Claus," he said, "where have you been?"

"Oh," said Mrs. Claus, "well, I—"

"Never mind," said Santa. "You can explain later."

When they got into the house, Mrs. Claus's mouth dropped open. Tinsel and cranberries were strung all over the living room! The lights on the big Christmas tree were blinking on and off. The elves brought out a steaming pot of cocoa and a plate of cookies.

"Why, Santa," said Mrs. Claus, "this is wonderful."

Santa laughed. "The elves told me about Davey's puppy. We wanted to welcome you home."

He hugged and kissed her. "Merry Christmas," he said.

"Merry Christmas," sang the elves.

Mrs. Claus smiled and sighed. "Merry Christmas, everyone," she said.